# WHEN THE JUNGLES WHISPER!

# WHEN THE JUNGLES WHISPER!

PREETHI MENON

HarperCollins*Children'sBooks*

First published in India in 2022 by HarperCollins Children's Books
An imprint of HarperCollins *Publishers*
Building No. 10, Tower A, 4th Floor, DLF Cyber City,
Phase II, Gurugram, 122002, India
www.harpercollins.co.in

2 4 6 8 10 9 7 5 3



P-ISBN: 9789394407350
E-ISBN: 9789394407428



Typeset in Minion Pro 13 pt/18 pt
by Veena, Bookwatch
Cover design by Isha Nagar

Printed and bound at
Thomson Press (India) Ltd

To,

my Dad

who had a great sense of humour

and who loved writing mono-act scripts

which I would enthusiastically enact!

# CONTENTS

## FOREWORD

# When the Jungles Whisper, You Better Listen!

My father, the renowned writer Shivarama Karanth, did not believe in formal schooling. He often remarked that 'schools are slaughterhouses of children's curiosity'. He was inspired by Maria Montessori's vision of nurturing creativity and curiosity in every child by making learning seem like play. In the early 1930s, he established his 'Balavana' (children's forest), an experimental school set in a six-acre wooded lot between the Mangalore coast and the Western Ghats of Karnataka. Before I was born, that school had shut down for lack of parental support for such radical experiments in pedagogy. However, all three of my siblings and I still became guinea pigs in the Balavana experiment. Boy, was I a happy guinea pig!

Until I joined the high school directly at sixth grade, exploring and playing in the woods of Balavana all day was the education I got, except for an hour of Kannada and maths my mother taught us. However, Balavana did have a fabulous library with many books on wildlife and nature. The love and curiosity for wildlife were firmly seeded in me.

An aunt who was fond of me taught me birdwatching. As I grew up, I was saddened to see that my schoolmates and college friends missed so much in life because the child's inherent curiosity about nature in them had been snuffed out in the relentless pursuit of scholastic grades, or a hankering for gadgets.

I am glad to see that things are now changing, albeit slowly. Books, the internet and visual media are bringing nature closer to children again. And, outside of the still somewhat dreary school curricula, writers with an interest in nature, like the author Preethi Menon, are enriching the lives of students with fascinating tales about wildlife and wild lands of our truly spectacular country.

Another thing has changed. At least in some nature reserves of India, the relentless hunting of the past, which had made wildlife scarce and shy, has declined. Children can now actually visit wildlife sanctuaries and see wild animals in natural habitats.

In this book, Preethi Menon tries to ignite that essential first spark of curiosity about wildlife in children of 6–9 years. It is a collection of 26 stories. Preethi writes lucidly and with verve to bond her readers to these wonderful animals. She adopts a unique model of storytelling where each of these species becomes the central character in the tale. Yet, these are 'serious' children's stories where the overarching theme of species endangerment lurks in the shadows. The central characters in her tales include endangered birds ranging from the Bengal florican and the Himalayan quail to the white-rumped vulture. The cast of characters also includes mammals like the Gangetic dolphin, reptiles like the gharial or even tiny amphibians like the Xanthophryne tigerina toad. And, of course, charismatic species such as elephants, lions and tigers are there too.

The author also successfully captures the flavour and essence of the diversity of landscapes, the terrain, forests, wetlands and other habitats in which these creatures survive, even managing to weave bits of local culture into her tales. Most importantly, these stories are laced with optimism and hope, something we really need if we are to save these species for the generations to come.

I am sure this book will be well received and avidly read by all children. I also hope, when these kids are asleep, their parents, and teachers, will also open its covers and listen to these whispers of the jungle. They will be enriched by the passion and knowledge Preethi lovingly shares with their wards.

K. ULLAS KARANTH, PhD<br>Centre for Wildlife Studies

# INTRODUCTION

It would be wonderful if wild animals could tell us their personal stories, what they like, what they're afraid of and what they think of us, human beings. Well, they can't but Preethi Menon takes us on a delightful journey through the lives and adventures of wild creatures across the great expanse of India with its wonderful and scenic deserts, oceans, rivers and forests.

When Kanna and Molu go home on vacation they stay with their grandmother, Ammuma, in a beautiful village surrounded by hills and farms and forests. She knows exactly how to keep them happy and every evening reads to them from the book *When the Jungles Whisper*. The book is full of exciting and amusing stories about animals large and small.

Some are critically endangered, like Gowri the long-snouted, fish-eating crocodile called the gharial who lives in the Chambal river in the north. She needs a safe place to lay her eggs and raise her young. Rivers are being ruined by sand mining and pollution and luckily the Chambal is now a protected sanctuary for gharial, river dolphins, rare turtles and the waterbirds that use islands in the river for safe nesting.

Another endangered creature is Bansi the Bengal florican who goes to school and meets many fellow birds like herons, pelicans, swifts and bush quail. Kanna and Molu are fascinated and want to know why and how birds become endangered and what can be done to help them survive. Ammuma encourages them to read about endangered species and how their problems can be solved.

Chandrika is a king cobra who was unlucky enough to be captured and put into a woven basket by a snake charmer and as he played his flute he'd make her sit up and look dangerous. She gets rescued and stays in a spacious cage in a zoo where she impresses the many visitors who come to gape at her. She notices a little girl staring at her in awe and though they can't speak to each other Chandrika sits up and spreads her magnificent hood and makes a permanent impression on the little girl. Snakes are beautiful, and not scary at all!

There are numerous other short stories of animals with personalities, from deer in the Himalayas and rodents in the Andaman Islands to toads in the Western Ghats. They take you on a tour of India's wild places to meet some of the vast variety of mammals, birds, reptiles and amphibians that share their lives with us. Here is a perfect reading experience for bedtime or anytime!

ROMULUS WHITAKER
renowned wildlife conservationist

# How It All Began ...

*The moon sat snugly in the sky. A whiff of the sweet jasmine scent wafted through the children's bedroom window. In the distance, the mountains stood silent and magnificent.*

*How different life in Grandma's village was! Kanna and Molu loved spending their holidays wandering about the countryside, plucking, squishing and eating juicy mangoes. Afternoons were devoted to diving competitions with cousins in the pond nearby. Evenings after supper were the most exciting. Their grandma, who they called Ammuma, would read to them wonderful tales of the birds and animals that brought the jungles in India alive – tales of endangered species.*

*'If jungles are home for the animals, how can they be in danger?' Molu asked.*

*'People hunt them for their meat or skin, and sometimes for sport. They lose their habitat because the land is used to grow crops or build urban spaces. As a result, many of these species are on the brink of extinction,' Ammuma explained.*

*'So what are we doing to protect them, Ammu?'*

*'Lots of conservation efforts are being made by people who care. We'll find out more in these stories.'*

*They read every night until the clock struck ten. Ammuma would then announce, 'It's lights-out time' and kiss them goodnight. Their favourite pastime before falling asleep was to imagine themselves on a jumbo trail exploring these jungles. On one such night, Kanna noticed through sleep-laden eyes, tiny lights flickering outside their bedroom window. He must find out what was happening.*

*'Molu, look at this,' he whispered, moving closer to the window.*

*Molu hurried over and almost tripped on the rug. 'Fireflies!' she gasped wide-eyed, as they made zigzag and criss-cross patterns in the air. After a two-minute glowing performance, they flitted away.*

*'Let's go after them,' Kanna said. Tiptoeing out of the house, they followed the fireflies to the end of the path leading to their gate. Crickets had begun to make a racket. The fireflies hovered in the air for a moment before they vanished into the thick night.*

*'Ssshhh ... Did you hear that?' Kanna and Molu strained their ears to listen.*

*Could they hear the jungles whispering?*

*Let's begin our journey from Bandipur forest in the southern state of Karnataka, where our first tale of the ASIAN ELEPHANT is set.*

# Anju's Awesome Adventure

Anju sighed deeply as she waved her trunk at birds flying around her. She had been lonely ever since her best friend, Janu, had left for another forest. Her mother, Ammini, gently nudged her as if to ask what the matter was.

'I miss Janu. I wish I could see her,' Anju said with another sigh so deep that it blew off the birds that were sitting on her trunk.

'Are you ready for an adventure?' Ammini asked. Anju couldn't believe her ears! The next morning, they were on their way to meet Janu, along with Anju's aunt.

'Will Janu remember me? Can she flap her ears? Does she swim? I bet she can't dance the Jumbo-Jiggy-Wiggy.'

'Relax, we'll find out soon. Besides, you don't want Janu to think you're blowing your own trumpet,' smiled Ammini, as she plucked a bunch of bananas and tucked them into her mouth in one fluid motion.

Anju continued to jabber like an express train about the games she played, such as 'I Spy' with the squirrels, and 'Tickle My Trunk' with

the birds. Their trek took them through many secret paths in the jungle.

'How will we remember our way back?' Anju asked her mother.

'Elephants have the best memories. We remember everything,' replied Ammini.

Along the way, the two jumbos made low rumbling noises to communicate with other elephants in the jungle. By doing so, they got important information – how to avoid danger, when to change direction, where to get water and so on.

Suddenly, Ammini stopped in her tracks. She could sense danger.

'Ssshhh … be quiet and stay still.' Through the thick grass, Anju saw the fiery orange stripes and rippling muscles of Agni the ferocious tiger. This was her territory. Ammini and Agni looked at each other for a moment. No one moved. After a few tense moments, Agni walked away quietly. That was close!

Just before reaching River Kabini, they saw Janu's mom waiting at the clearing. She ambled forward to greet her dear friends. After a trunkful of greetings, they rested for a while. Anju looked shyly at Janu, tongue-tied. She forgot everything she had thought she would say to her old friend. So much for the famed elephant memory!

'Can we play near the bamboo?' Janu asked, breaking the awkward silence. Janu's mom and Ammini agreed and reminded them of safety rules.

'Remember, if you see snakes, just step aside and walk away.'

The two calves trumpeted 'Yeh!' and ran towards the river. Anju and Janu were going to play hide and seek, roll in the mud, squirt water over each other, do the Jumbo-Jiggy-Wiggy and …

What an awesome adventure!

*'The Jumbo-Jiggy-Wiggy! Hey, we should try that,' Kanna said excitedly as he secretly wished he could roll in the mud as well.*

*Now we will go to the North East, in the Brahmaputra Delta, the home of the critically endangered BENGAL FLORICAN.*

# Bansi's Bubbly Buddies

Bansi gave a sharp chirp at the crack of dawn. 'Cheep! Cheep! Wake up, Dada. I don't want to be late on my big day!' He impatiently pecked around, eager to leave.

Bansi lived in the tall grasslands. Ever so often, his family moved from place to place because their homes kept disappearing. Humans occupied their land to make fields to sow crops. It made Bansi very sad, but that was about to change.

As Bansi and Dada approached the opening of a grove hidden deep in the dense grass, where humans can't reach, Bansi heard the shrill trill of hundreds of birds. Some were fidgeting, some flitting, some fussing. What a hullabaloo! Bansi was so excited, he didn't notice the butterflies fluttering in his tummy. He barely heard his dada tweet him goodbye. He was already making his way through the cacophony.

'Welcome to Sangeeth Kindergarten. I'm Miss Bhavna, your music teacher,' warbled a colourful Blyth's kingfisher, looking picture-perfect under a canopy of flowers. Her coat seemed to be woven out of

Welcome!
I'm Miss Bhavna.
Sangeeth kindergarten
Hello! I am Bansi!
Hiiiii!
I am Madhuri!
I am Dhuni
Hello! I am Shruti!

rainbow fabric. Bansi spotted a bird, whose head looked like it had been dipped in a chimney full of smoke. A sooty-headed bulbul, her name was Swara. They twittered for a while before he flew to meet another Bengal florican.

In their symphony class, Miss Bhavna dreamily harped, 'We're the world's most gifted musicians. It's not what we tweet, but how we tweet that creates a flutter. Let's open our beaks wide and sing "with feeling".'

*'Flit float fly, cheep, cheep,*
*hearts full of joy, beep beep!*
*Kuhu pihu kuhu pihu,*
*chippy chippy chin chiyuu!'*

Shruti the spot-billed pelican opened her beak to sing, but it was so long that it struck Dhun the dark-rumped swift, in the eye. 'Chin-chiyuu-ooww!' he cried out in pain, which disturbed the rhythm of the song. Madhuri the Manipur bush quail, couldn't stop giggling. Seeing her, everyone broke into titters.

Funny thing about time, it flies just when you are having fun. By the end of the day, Bansi had struck a chord with many new friends.

'I love Sangeeth Kindergarten. I hope we won't have to move again, Dada,' Bansi chirped happily. He snuggled in a cosy corner after a supper of delicious berries and seeds, while the streams gently gurgled a lullaby.

*'I love Sangeeth Kindergarten too,' Molu said, humming a tune as they got ready for bed.*

*'Flit float fly, cheep cheep!'*

*Follow our slithering trail to Patna, in Bihar, where the KING COBRA resides.*

# Charming Chandrika's Chat

Chandrika lay coiled in the far corner, looking lazily at groups of humans passing by. Over nine feet long, she was one of the main attractions of the zoo. Years ago, Chandrika had been rescued from a snake charmer in a village nearby and brought to the zoo in a rucksack. Was she sad? On the contrary, she felt the opposite.

Each time the humans stopped at her cage, they said the name on the label outside, 'The King Cobra', as if reading it aloud would make her break into a snake dance. Some gaped, and some made faces. How silly!

But there was one little girl who looked at the cobra in awe. 'What's your story?' she seemed to ask.

Chandrika was reminded of that fateful afternoon. She had been upset because the other snakes had called her 'crafty cobra'. She slithered out of her hole, not paying attention to her mother, who warned her of the dangers lurking around. 'Names cannot hurt you, my dear, but humans can. So beware.'

NO FLASH
PHOTOGRAPHY
ALLOWED.

Chandrika saw humans in the distance and stopped. It happened in a flash. Something fell on her and everything went dark. Oh no! She was trapped in a wicker basket. From then on, whenever her master played the pungi pipe, she would sense the vibrations and emerge from the basket, swaying slowly. She couldn't help it. Humans thought she was dancing to the snake-charmer's tune, but this was Chandrika's way of defending herself. So tiring. In her new home though, she could relax, coil up and chill out!

Now, a slight movement brought Chandrika to the present moment. She glided to the window and stopped in front of the girl. Lifting her head, she spread her hood in all its glory. The crowd gasped and cameras flashed feverishly. *Klitch – Klitch – Klitch!* Chandrika felt uncomfortable with the bright lights. The girl was annoyed and pointed to the sign outside. The lights stopped flashing.

Maybe humans would look kindly upon snakes, instead of seeing them as scary, evil reptiles. Even the mighty elephants respected the cobra. They would quietly step aside without harming her.

For a moment, Chandrika found herself alone with the girl. She swayed gently as if dancing to some forgotten tune. 'Charmed to meet you!' hissed Chandrika.

Their eyes met before she slithered back to her corner.

*There was a faraway look in the children's eyes as Ammuma finished reading.*

*'Are cobras endangered?'*

*'Good question, Kanna! You can research that topic,' Ammuma replied.*

*Let's take you to the mountains of Uttarakhand where the rivers Ganga and Yamuna meet to see the GANGES RIVER DOLPHINS.*

# Divya's Dandy Dance

Divya poked her snout out of the water and surveyed the banks of River Ganga. Empty. When the banks were full of humans, she would wait for the right moment, leap in the air and flip, splashing water over all who gathered there. What a naughty dolphin! You could hear her clicking in delight as she swam away, dancing her special jig. *Wiggle-Whistle, Leap-Flip, Dive-Splash, Wiggle-Whistle!*

'Come on, let's play *Fastest Flip*,' Divya said to her friends Devi and Darshan.

'Nah ... the water isn't clean,' said Darshan, scrunching his snout.

It was true. The once clear and fresh waters of her hometown Devprayag had become soiled with decades of human use. But, that didn't dampen Divya's spirits.

'We could fall sick,' Darshan continued, looking at Devi for reinforcement.

'Or worse, we could get caught in a fisherman's net,' Devi said hastily. 'Remember what happened to Dipa?'

How could Divya forget? Dipa's long snout had got entangled in a fishing net. Divya had cried a river of tears when she heard about the tragedy.

'There are no fishing boats now. A virus is going around keeping humans at bay. Haven't you noticed?' Divya could see that the two dolphins were thinking. She continued, 'We'll stay clear of busy and polluted areas using our echolocation* skills. Let's go. It's *Fastest Flip* time!'

That did the trick. Dolphins can navigate underwater using echolocation. Divya's uncle had once said that huge machines called submarines copied their style of communication. Isn't it great how they inspired humans?

The three set off on their adventure. Divya had a plan but she wasn't going to reveal it yet. On their way, they saw fishing boats and quickly changed direction to avoid danger. A few miles later, they saw river rafts rushing towards the rapids. The three dolphins swam along with the rafts, flipping and splashing with the current. The humans seemed thrilled. They clapped and cheered with glee.

'We should head back,' Darshan said.

'What? Don't be a killjoy. Besides, Jancy's home is just a few hours away. Let's surprise him!'

Divya swam ahead before they could reply. Devi and Darshan looked at each other for a moment.

Then, with a sly click of his tongue, Darshan asked, 'Shall we dance the *Wiggle-Whistle?*'

*'I like Divya's spirit!' Kanna said bright-eyed. 'She's adventurous.'*

*'Do you think Darshan and Devi will join her?' Ammuma asked.*

*'I would go,' Kanna said, 'doing the Wiggle-Whistle!'*

*They laughed at that. Ammuma announced it was lights-out time.*

---

* a technique of sending calls through sound waves that reflect information which helps dolphins and whales communicate, navigate and hunt underwater

*The desert of Rajasthan is where our jumbo trail leads us next. Here we can hope to spot the STEPPE EAGLE.*

# Eklavya's Extreme Escapade

Eklavya soared high into the desert sky. With his large outstretched wings, he looked regal. His keen eyes missed nothing. When he looked at you, you could feel your knees wobbling! His killer looks were enough to make all creatures go scrambling for safety.

'It's that eagle on the hunt again!' the rabbits cried out, warning each other, as they ran for their lives to escape Eklavya's powerful razor-sharp talons.

Like many migratory birds, Eklavya flew into India every November to escape the icy cold winters of Russia and stayed until March. He liked travelling. It broadened his horizons.

Flying high, Eklavya remembered an incident that had happened five years ago. He was in his eyrie*, waiting for his mum to return with food when he saw two tiny robins playing a game.

'Truth or Dare?' asked the first robin.

'Truth,' replied the second.

---

* eagle's nest

'How many worms did you catch this morning?'

'Five!'

'That's a lie!' said the first robin. 'Now it's my turn. I'll take a dare.'

'All right,' said the second. 'I dare you to fly up to that eagle and say hello!'

Eklavya had an idea. He would meet the second robin halfway! He hadn't started his flying lessons yet, but how hard could it be? Inching forward, he put one talon in front of the eyrie and looked down. He shuddered. The ground seemed like a bottomless hole.

Giving his juvenile wings a flutter, Eklavya took a deep breath through his tiny angular nostrils. 'OK, here goes.' He was about to throw himself into the air when he heard a screech, 'EKKU NOOO!' Luckily, he was pushed back into the nest in the nick of time.

'Phew, that was close!' his mum Ekta said, heaving a sigh of relief. 'What were you thinking? You are not ready to fly yet.'

Eklavya learned an important lesson that day – never to get ahead of himself. He would pass on the lesson to his eaglet one day.

'Thankfully, I lived to fly another day,' he thought, while soaring in the desert sky, alone.

*Truth or Dare ... Hmm, interesting game for Kanna and Molu. Ammuma knew exactly what they were thinking!*

*We are off to sunny Goa, to see the ANAIMALAI FLYING FROGS of the Western Ghats. They have arrived there for a special occasion.*

# Freddie's Froggie Fanfare

Freddie was ever so ready! He was going to propose to his sweetheart Frida. If she agreed, which Freddie hoped she would, he'd have to start the wedding preparations on the double.

His mind raced to the first time they met. It was love at first sight. Frida's emerald-green skin and big cup-shaped eyes were so striking. Freddie instantly decided she was the one for him.

Freddie had pulled out all the stops to make the day memorable. He made a mossy ring and arranged for an orchestra to play after he popped the question. The menu was carefully chosen – a variety of crunchy-munchy moths, delicious dragonflies and crispy crickets would be served as starters. The main course was spicy Spider Sorpotel and Rodent Recheado, rounded off with Beetle Bebinca dessert. Freddie's mouth watered just thinking about the menu!

On the big day, everything took off with utmost precision – the cuisine, the decoration, the music. Freddie entered in style, flying from a tree and flopping onto the lilypad, bearing the ring. When he asked

tap

Frida to marry him, there was not a single dry eye in the audience.

Frida said, 'Yes' and Freddie cried, 'Woo-hoo' in delight, amidst cheers.

And now, for the grand finale. Freddie was going to sing. He leapt onto the branch of a nearby tree in a split second. The bandmaster gave the signal. On cue, the orchestra began playing.

> *'Jinga jaenga jinga jaenga jinga jaenga jing jing*
> *Rampam poey ... rampam poe'*

Freddie opened his frog mouth and in an explosion of pure love, he … croaked! What was THAT? A stunned silence followed. Frida's mouth was open in shock. 'He should never sing in public,' she thought. Luckily, a fly came buzzing by. Perfect timing. She caught it with a flick of her tongue. Gulp!

Just then, the pitter-patter of raindrops flopped on the floor. Within minutes, the whole ground turned into large mud pools with frogs flying and grooving to the beat of the rain.

Everyone forgot about Freddie's disaster. The rains turned out to his advantage making it the best Froggie engagement ever!

*'Aren't frogs meant to croak anyway?' Molu asked, a bit miffed at Frida's reaction.*

*Kanna was thinking about the menu. Sorpotel was one of his favourite dishes, but maybe not with spiders.*

*Follow us on the Gangetic Plains, cutting through ravines and into the National Chambal Sanctuary in Madhya Pradesh, to meet the GHARIALS.*

# Gowri Gears Up!

Gowri basked in the afternoon sun with a newspaper on the sandy banks of the Chambal river, catching up on the latest news. She and Gaby had just finished a delicious meal of fish. Now she needed her Vitamin D, as she was expecting babies. They had found the perfect spot to lay her eggs, right where she was! Water moved in a slow, lazy way as if it was taking in all the lovely sights of nature, unhurried.

Why did the front page of the newspaper always carry sad news?

*River Beds Dry Up* read one headline. *All Fish Fished Out!* screamed another, all this because of overfishing and illegal sand mining. Hmm, that's fishy! She had had some for breakfast. Gowri turned the pages to the section titled *Endangered Species in Chambal Sanctuaries.* Her species was on top of the list. She read about the conservation measures being adopted for minimizing the impact of illegal sand mining and riverbed farming. Steps were also being taken to protect the red-crowned roofed turtle, by creating temporary homes beside their nesting sites.

Good, things are changing. Humans are finally doing something about the situation. Heaving a sigh of relief, Gowri got ready for her nap.

She snuggled in her sunny spot, and was about to doze off when she sensed an unfamiliar movement. Oh, bother! Who could that be? In the distance, her turtle friend Tarika was ambling towards her. On seeing her, Gowri remembered the day they had met a couple of years ago. She was swimming near the riverbed when she felt a slight tickle in her tail. Thinking it was a juicy fish, she swiftly turned to catch it. Blonk! She had bitten a hard turtle shell instead. Gowri was lucky to have her teeth intact and Gaby laughed till he shed crocodile tears!

'Tarika, what a surprise!' Gowri exclaimed, seeing her friend. Tarika beamed as she handed Gowri a bouquet of gorgeous red palash flowers

and a box of ber.

'How thoughtful of you!' Gowri remarked, her face glowing with joy.

'I thought I'd drop by. There's good news. I'm going to have babies,' Tarika announced.

'That makes two of us,' Gowri piped in gleefully.

They sat by the freshwaters, sharing their funny stories and laughing until the sun sank into the ravines taking down the fading orange hue of sunset.

*'What a weird friendship! I'm sure in real life Gowri would have gobbled up Tarika,' Molu thought out loud.*

*'Yeah, but the point is making friends with people who are different from you!' Ammuma was happy. They were engaging with the stories.*

*Our next tale is of HANGUL THE RED STAG and is set against the snow-capped mountains of Kashmir, India's crowning glory.*

# Hasan's High House

Hasan cocked his ear to one side, ready to run at the slightest hint of danger. Had he imagined the sound of feet treading in the snow? Hiding among the tall trees, Hasan saw the silhouette of antlers in the twilight. There was only one other hangul living in his neighbourhood.

'Armaan, is that you?' he whispered, letting out a misty blue spray of cold air from his mouth.

There was an eerie silence before Armaan answered, 'Hasan, thank heavens you're safe!'

Hasan was a 'hangul', the local name for a Kashmir red stag. He stood five feet from his shoulders with magnificent antlers that had sixteen points in them. Over the years, Hasan had learned to be alert and rely on his senses. He could dodge even the snow leopard, but humans were his greatest fear. They were unpredictable and did not follow the rules of the animal world.

'Welcome back,' Hasan said in relief, coming out of his hiding to greet Armaan.

Armaan had fled a year ago when his friends in the valley were being attacked by humans. Later on, the hanguls heard of conservation measures which allowed them to roam about safely. That's when they started returning.

'Any news of the other stags?' Armaan asked. He had missed his home, the mountains, rivers and valleys.

'I hear they're fine, and will return shortly for the "Hangul Homecoming" here in Dachigam,' Hasan said.

The two long-lost friends had much to catch up on. Hasan and Armaan had their differences and had even got into a huge fight, locking horns over lovely Heena once! Part of growing up.

'You're just in time for supper. Come, my mother will be so glad to see you. We can talk over a hot cup of kahwa.'

They walked to Hasan's home high up in the mountains. A trillion stars twinkled their approval over the friends' reunion in the silvery-white paradise.

A pair of emerald green eyes stared unblinkingly from behind the trees. The snow leopard watched the two hanguls as they trudged up. He knew that Hasan was quick to sense danger. He would have to bide his time.

*'I want to go to Kashmir and see a hangul,' Kanna said wistfully.*

*'Me too,' Molu chipped in. 'I love its horns. Where are we headed next?'*

*'Depends on where you want to go on your jumbo trail,' Ammuma replied.*

*Moving on to west India, our next tale is set in the Gir National Park of Gujarat where the INDIAN/ASIATIC LIONS roam wild and free.*

# Izzy's Impish Idea

Izzy slipped from the tree and fell on his bottom. While his sisters were out on their practice hunt with Mama, he preferred exploring other options. One last try, Izzy thought and started the climb. A couple of meddlesome monkeys watched him intently and shook the branches to distract him. The leaves tickled Izzy's nostrils.

'Aaah, aaah ... achooooo!' Oops! Izzy lost his balance and fell again with a thud. When he got up, he found himself looking straight into his father's stern face. Oh boy! Izzy was in big trouble. Aunt Ira stood behind him with a concerned expression on her face.

'Izzy, why aren't you with your sisters for the practice hunt?' Indra asked.

'I -er … I -er …' Izzy stammered.

'That's right, you erred,' Indra said. 'Lions don't climb trees. None of that monkey business for us. You're lucky you didn't get hurt. Run along now.'

'But, Pa, could I just …'

Izzy's father Indra replied with a mighty roar that thundered through the forest. A nearby herd of sambars perked up their ears, ready to run. Monkeys in the midst of cackling over Izzy's fall fell silent. A great Indian bustard, pecking around for insects, flew off in fright. Izzy cowered in fear.

Indra was known far and wide for his strength and huge pride of lions. Although he was a mighty lion, he could not withstand attacks from humans or defend against the loss of their habitat. For many years, Asiatic lions had roamed far and wide. Today, they were forced to stay within the forests of southwest Gujarat because humans had taken up most of their space. It was unfair!

'Don't be so hard on Izzy,' Ira said. 'He'll follow in your footsteps one day.' Ira tried to lighten the moment. Indra grunted.

'Your three female hunters are showing great promise already. You won't have to worry about food. We do all the hard work,' Ira said.

'That's true,' Indra agreed with a slight smile. 'But I protect my pride, which is hard work too. Izzy will learn that from me.' He looked at his son who was sulking under the tree. Perhaps Ira was right. Izzy would learn when the time comes.

'All right, one last time and then off you go,' Indra said. No sooner had he completed the sentence than Izzy began climbing the tree. His impish idea may work after all!

*'Izzy is lucky his father didn't get too mad at him,' Molu said with relief.*

*'Yeah, one needs to explore one's options!' Kanna said, and they both laughed.*

*Our next trail is on a different mode of transport. We are headed to the South Andaman Islands where the JENKINS'S SHREWS are found.*

# Jancy's Jolly Jubilee

Jancy opened the front door of his beach house. 'Mommy, I'm home!' he shouted excitedly as a waft of wonderful aroma hit his nostrils.

'Get ready, son,' Mommy Julie said. 'Our porch needs a little touch-up.'

All afternoon, Jancy's brothers Jim and Joe had been working to get his birthday party set up; blowing balloons, setting tables, arranging music playlists, and the final touch – a photo booth.

By 5 p.m., his friends had started arriving. Apart from fellow shrews, he had invited two special feathered friends from the neighbouring islands. Since transportation wasn't a problem, Nina the Nicobar pigeon and Natty the Narcondam hornbill had gladly flown in. Like him, they too were endangered and rarely socialized. It would be nice to meet up.

Mommy Julie laid out party snacks on the table. A plate of cheese cubes was placed in the centre. Yikes! Jancy winced. The cheese triggered a scary memory. On one of his late-night sniff-outs, an enticing whiff had led Jancy into the backyard of a human house.

Leftovers were piled in a corner next to the trash bag. Strange. They were usually in the trash bag. Then he saw it – cheese! Jancy moved greedily towards it when someone squawked. He would have walked into a trap had Nina the Nicobar pigeon not warned him!

'Let the party begin,' Joe twittered as Jim played music. Jancy jigged joyfully while the birds circled around him, matching his moves. The sky was turning orange, making their feathers glisten in the sunset. Mommy Julie brought out the cake shaped like the Andaman Islands. Yummy! Natty led the jingle.

*For he's a jolly good Jancy,*
*That's true and plain as we can see*
*A happy-go-lucky shrew is he,*
*I'm sure you'll all agree!*

Everyone had a generous helping of the delicious cake. It was time for some pictures at the photo booth. What a lovely backdrop of the sea and the setting sun!

'Say cheese!' Nina squawked, winking at Jancy who winked back. In the distance, Jancy saw a familiar snout poking out of the sea. Was it his imagination? Suddenly, Divya his dolphin friend leapt in the air doing her wiggle-whistle and splashed water all over the guests!

'Happy birthday, Jancyyy!' It was a jolly jubilee indeed.

*'What a party! I want a photo booth for my birthday,' sighed Molu, longingly.*

*'And I want a beach party,' Kanna added, 'with lots of popcorn and sausages.'*

*Ammuma let them discuss their dream parties before she switched off the lights.*

*Far up north, in Punjab, roams the braveheart blackbuck or the KALA HIRAN in Abohar Wildlife Sanctuary, where we head for our next tale.*

# Kuldeep's Kind Kindred

Kuldeep hardly slept a wink. He tossed and turned the whole night, eagerly waiting for daybreak. What could be the reason?

A few days ago, Kuldeep had come home in tears.

'What's wrong, puttar?' asked Grandpa Kiranjit anxiously. Kuldeep was such a happy hiran that it broke Kiranjit's heart to see his grandkid sobbing.

'Is it true that our species are decreasing, Dadu? My friend Karan told me he lost his cousins. They were poached.' Kuldeep sniffed as his eyes brimmed with fresh tears. Kiranjit was taken aback.

'There, there. No need to worry. We have many safe places created by humans now,' Kiranjit replied as honestly as he could. Kuldeep seemed comforted by this news. Kiranjit had an idea to cheer up his grandkid.

'Why don't we do something different this weekend? How does a visit to the Harike Bird Sanctuary sound? We'll start at the crack of dawn.'

No wonder Kuldeep couldn't sleep! Even before the birds had begun stirring, Kuldeep was awake and wide-eyed with excitement. On their way, they saw the most extraordinary sunrise. It was as if the sun could not hold his rays any longer and splashed them across the sky, turning it into a colourful canvas!

The Harike Bird Sanctuary was beyond Kuldeep's wildest imagination. There were a thousand birds cooing and cawing, whistling and whooping, some taking off, others landing, some flying in patterns, others squabbling for food. He read aloud tongue-twister names of different species from the list on the board.

'Black-bellied terns, mew gull, lesser whistling duck, moustached warbler ...' A bird with a moustache and a whistling duck? How fascinating!

Kuldeep's head bobbed up, down, left, right. His eyes went in all directions at once. In one gigantic swoop, hundreds of red-crested pochard ducks dived into the water, turning the wetlands into a dancing fountain. What an incredible experience! 'Imagine, these migratory birds have flown in from as far as Siberia,' Dadu said.

Kuldeep bleated in delight and rubbed his head against his grandpa.

'Awesome, Dadu! Such a big bird park for them to play in.' Dadu was the kindest blackbuck ever. That night, Kuldeep slipped into a deep, joyful sleep, dreaming of flying with the birds and diving with the ducks. Whoosh! Whizz! Wirrrr!

*'Even I will dream of flying with the birds,' sighed Molu with a dreamy look in her eyes.*

*Kanna's mind was racing. He was going to dedicate some time to research these birds the next morning.*

*Our jumbo trail takes us once again to the rainforests in the Silent Valley National Park of Kerala, where we meet the LION-TAILED MACAQUE.*

# Lila's Lucky Life

Lila swung from one branch to another one humid afternoon.

'What's so special about us, Amma?' Lila asked her mother, not really waiting for an answer. Lila knew why she was special. She had heard that they were one of the few remaining primates of their kind in the world. Except for a few humans now and then visiting to stare at them, they were hardly disturbed in the forest.

'That's the hundredth time you are asking me this question,' her mother Lalita puffed with irritation. 'Lila, where are you going?'

'I'll be back before dusk, Amma. I promise,' Lila screeched as she swung her long tail and glided smoothly onto the next tree.

'It's going to rain soon. Your silvery mane will get damp.' Lalita was not happy with Lila. Why couldn't she look after her gorgeous mane? 'Aiyooo, what do I do with her?' Lalita mumbled, shaking her head and going back to scratching her legs.

Lila disappeared into the forest. Her friends, Neeli the Nilgiri langur and Benny the bonnet macaque, would be waiting for her by the river

Kunthi. They were going to pick their special snack, vediplavu*. The name is a mouthful, but who cares. The fruit is so juicy and there's plenty for the taking.

Forty metres high with a belly full of fruit, Lila smacked her lips and sighed in contentment.

'You know what's different about this forest?' Neeli asked, burping loudly.

'What?' Benny was swinging from the tree branch, up to his usual monkey tricks.

'Three guesses,' she said.

'Leopards are friendly?'

Neeli shook her head.

'Monkeys don't have lice in their hair?'

'Euuu, no!'

'Deer climb trees here.'

'Uff! No! It's the lack of sound, you dumbo! No noisy cicadas** around here. That's why it's called the Silent Valley. Duh!' Neeli said, rolling her eyes.

Lila giggled. She was enjoying the conversation. The three had similar skills, especially for climbing trees, and yet they were different in size, shape and features. Next, she would reach out to Mani the Malabar squirrel, who would show them where the ripe vediplavu were.

Good home, great friends, yummy food … yes! Lila was feeling lucky indeed.

*'Trick question. Speaking of deer, which came first, deer sambar or dish sambar?' Kanna asked, his eyes glinting mischievously.*

*'Huh?' Molu scratched her head while Ammuma had a hearty laugh.*

* plant species of jackfruit in evergreen forests

** insects that make noise by rubbing their legs together

*We move towards central India, into Udanti Sitanadi Tiger Reserve in the state of Chhattisgarh, where the MOUSE DEER lives.*

# Meera's Magical Moment

Meera the mouse deer was going back to her birthplace, Udanti forest. She was tiny compared to other deer species, like a little brown button, cute but easy prey for predators. The journey from Tadoba Tiger Reserve to Udanti would be risky, but Meera had to follow her heart.

'So you thought you could leave without telling us?' Bittu said, frowning. Bittu was a wild buffalo, Meera's heavyweight buddy. 'We're tagging along. I'll protect you and when you get tired, I'll carry you on my back.' Bittu looked so earnest that Meera didn't have the heart to refuse.

'Bittu's right and I could do with a change of place,' said her other pal, Sonu the sambar deer. 'Besides, I need to find a mate.'

'We'll stick out like a sore thumb,' Meera laughed. 'A wild buffalo, a sambar, and a mouse deer riding piggyback!' It would indeed be an odd combination.

The three set off after sunset, taking advantage of the dark. They had to be alert at all times. Bittu's huge size and scary horns could ward

off even Maya the fierce tigress, who roamed around like a maharani! Sonu, too, could put his three-point antlers to good use when required, but what about humans? They attacked with deadly weapons. That was an eternal problem!

After a long and hard trek, the three reached Udanti forest at daybreak.

'Kiki-riku kiki-riku!' cooed a bulbul. From a branch nearby, a parakeet responded, 'Chichi-yuii chichi-yuii!' A couple of monkeys stopped gibbering to glance at the new kids on the block. Peeping timidly from behind the trees was a female sambar. A flying squirrel whizzed by from a tree branch, scattering loose wildflowers over Meera. One by one, the jungle life came out to greet the newcomers.

Meera's heart thumped wildly. Home at last! She turned to her friends. 'This is beyond my … where's Sonu? Where did he go?'

Bittu nodded towards the trees. Sonu was offering some berries to the female sambar. That was quick!

'Looks like he has found his mate!' Bittu said, smiling broadly.

For Meera, the heady smells of the forest and the warm welcome was truly a magical moment.

*There was silence when Ammuma finished this story. The only other sound was that of crickets outside. A gentle breeze blew through the open window. The kids sighed contentedly, feeling Meera's joy.*

*Perched on top of the Mukurthi National Park in the Nilgiri Biosphere Reserve, Tamil Nadu, our tale now spins around the NILGIRI TAHR.*

# Nimmi's Nippy Niche

Nimmi is trotting late. Trit-trot, trickety-trot, she makes her way up the treacherous path. The air is heavy with the scent of eucalyptus trees. A gust of cold wind pierces Nimmi's thoughts. Brushing the shrubs off her tawny grey back, she heads home.

At 8000-feet, Nimmi's home offers a 360-degree view of the Nilgiris, the beautiful blue mountains. The clouds look like whipped cream on azure blue skies. Day after day, Nimmi watches in amusement, and sometimes with boredom, the crowd of humans winding their way up the hills. They look like frenzied ants! She is careful not to be noticed, although on a few occasions she has had to bolt on seeing them.

Back home, two dear tahr friends, Mili from Munnar and Aditi from Anaimalai, reach in time for tea. Nimmi has picked the finest tea leaves and the choicest of herbs for the nibbles.

'What a stunning view!' Mili gasps, both from the excitement and from being breathless after the steep climb. Although tahrs are naturally nimble, Mili is clumsy. On her way up, she had slipped on the rocky

terrain and landed with a thud, legs in the air. Fortunately, no one was around to witness her fall. That's what she thought, but a bison grazing nearby had a good chuckle over it.

'Nimmi, your garden looks and smells heavenly!' Mili says, panting with the effort of being extra cautious. A blue-bearded bee-eater tweets in agreement.

'Truly breathtaking!' Aditi bleats.

'I'm thrilled out of my horns to have you both here!' Nimmi says, pouring them a hot pot of tea and a tray filled with savouries of herbs, and shoots of fresh bamboo.

Mili inches to the edge of the garden to smell the roses. 'Now, if you ask me, this patch ... aaaaah!' She slips and lands on her back, her legs flailing in the air. Poor Mili. Not again!

In the afternoon, the three tahrs catch up on the latest news.

'How's the weather in Anaimalai, Aditi?' Nimmi asks.

'Rather hot these days. They say climate change is the culprit.'

'And who's to blame for that?' Nimmi's question is the topic of discussion.

They talk until the indigo hues of the twilight hug the Nilgiris to a peaceful slumber.

*'I know someone clumsy like Mili,' Kanna said looking at Molu from the corner of his eye. She pretended to ignore the remark.*

*Let's move towards the eastern shores of Odisha where our story of the OLIVE RIDLEY TURTLES is based.*

# Onjali's Ongoing Operation

Onjali's journey to the Rushikulya river mouth had been smooth, free from human interaction. Apparently, a deadly flu was keeping them locked in their homes. Oh well, meddle with nature and that's what happens. Onjali turned her thoughts to her tribe – hundreds of olive ridley turtles were hurtling towards the shores of the sea.

Her besties, Ojal and Olly, had also travelled some thousand miles with her. It was the nesting season and they had returned for the arribadas*.

'Let's take a breather and wait for the others,' Onjali said, as she paused.

'What a journey!' Ojal sighed, wiping the sweat off her brow, and signalling her friends to rest for a bit. Most of them had been journeying all the way from Sri Lanka in the south. Other turtles were moving at a snail's pace with the effort of carrying eggs. They were home finally, at the same spot they had gathered last year.

* a Spanish term used for en masse laying of eggs by the turtle species

'Ah, the familiar sweet salty smell of the sea,' Olly poetically alliterated taking a deep breath. Ojal followed her gaze and did the same, breathing reverentially.

It was late March. The nesting time would take two months after their eggs were laid. Onjali and her friends were busy getting ready for the arrival of their babies.

'Have you thought of baby names?' Olly asked her friends.

'No, I'll wait until they hatch,' Onjali said. Ojal nodded in agreement. The soothing sound of the sea merged with the chirpy chiming of their chatter. They discussed turtle conservation schemes such as Operation Kachhapa*, which everyone agreed was a successful venture.

'I suppose there are some good humans out there who care for us,' Ojal said. They felt grateful for the human efforts to protect their nesting sites.

By May-end, baby turtles had hatched out of their eggs. Not all would be lucky to survive, but those who did would carry on their legacy.

'Isn't this the most amazing sight!' Onjali murmured, feeling dizzy with happiness as she watched hundreds of hatchlings making their way to the sea.

The moonlight shining on their backs made it seem like a reflection of the galaxy, sparkling with a million stars. How lovely our universe is!

*'Imagine returning to the exact spot every year! Amazing!' Ammuma said.*

*The children were lost in thought. Did the turtles have an internal GPS?*

* a Wildlife Protection Society of India (WPSI) initiative to protect turtles

*Let's catch a glimpse of the national bird, the PEACOCK, in action. We are going to take a stroll in Lodhi Gardens in the capital city of Delhi.*

# Prem's Perfect Plumes!

Prem was the chocolate boy of his neighbourhood. He was the prettiest peacock by far, and he knew it. Ahem, modesty was not one of Prem's virtues. At daybreak, he could be seen strutting around Lodhi Gardens in a self-appointed managerial role.

Prem found it hilarious that humans who frequented these gardens were often running after nothing in particular. This, he'd learned, was called jogging. Or they were twisting their bodies into strange positions. They called it yoga, an ancient Indian practice. Humans! Wonder what goes on inside their heads.

Prem liked to strut to a prime spot, give a little quiver before he dramatically opened his plumes*. Ta-da!

Wow! The profusion of blue, indigo blue, turquoise blue, sky blue, navy blue, was indeed a sight to behold. The vibrant shades dazzled his audience, throwing them into raptures. He hogged the limelight. Piyush had no such luck.

* feathers

'What a show-off!' Piyush scoffed, watching the whole drama unfurl from a champa tree. He secretly envied Prem.

'What's your problem? If the guy gets some thrills with his moves, why not?' Prabhat responded. He looked at the positive side of things.

'Why should he please the humans? He makes us look silly,' Piyush said, sulking.

'Oh, boo-hoo! Not everybody dances to please others. Sometimes, you want to do things for yourself. Besides, the peacock has style!' Prabhat shut him up.

Dark ominous clouds threatened to unleash their waters over Lodhi Gardens. It wasn't long before humans were scurrying for shelter. In the downpour, Prem stood alone and got ready to begin his routine.

'This is our chance. Let's seize the moment!' Prabhat said and flew over to Prem. 'It's showtime!' he screamed over the showers.

That morning, as the clouds burst open and the rain came crashing down, three peacocks opened their exquisite plumes and broke into a scintillating dance, shaking their feathers proudly to the rhythm of the showers. While humans took cover, peahens arrived to watch this stunning spectacle!

This time, Prem was not the only one they were interested in.

*'Hey, I like Prabhat's attitude. He seems like a cool guy!' Kanna said.*

*'I hope peacocks are not endangered,' Molu said as she remembered a bazaar at a local festival where peacock feathers were being sold.*

*We are going to Mussoorie next where the HIMALAYAN QUAIL used to live. They have not been sighted for over a century due to overhunting.*

# Quila's Quiet Quest

Quila thought the place looked familiar. She had been circling for hours, perching on different treetops, her head bobbing up and down as she surveyed the place carefully. There was a sense of deja vu, but she couldn't quite put her finger on it. Where was that bushy tree they would hide in?

She took a deep breath and inhaled the heady smells of the Himalayan forest. It transported her to a distant fading memory that she had buried in her head, afraid to let it come back. But today, she allowed her thoughts to wander down memory lane.

Quila and her partner Quinosh had flown through these very mountains many years ago. Nestled in the foothills was a beautiful eye-shaped lake. They flew low over its waters, skimming the surface now and then, taking turns to dip their wings in the icy waters.

It was not easy to spot them. They were both terribly shy. Often, they would hide from view. But when they did come out, it was easy to tell them apart. Quila had a yellow bill and yellow legs, while Quinosh

had a red bill with matching red legs! It was as if they were made for each other. Life was good.

The hills were much quieter then, Quila thought. She listened to the call of the laughing thrush as it flew somewhere close by. A treecreeper with its rather dull plumage was creeping around the next tree. It didn't seem to notice Quila. There was a sharp tweet from a nearby branch. Quila's gaze followed the sound. A Himalayan monal looked at her with a strange expression as if trying to read Quila's mind. Quila felt the bird's anxiety.

An unpleasant sound drifted through the woods, getting increasingly louder with each second. Quila's tiny heart raced like the barking dogs. She heard the shuffling of human feet, then suddenly a loud BANG!

The forest fell silent. It was almost deafening for Quila. Struck by a sudden realization, she flew down to the weeping willow tree by the lake and sat on the tallest branch. It all came back to her. She remembered why the place looked familiar.

She was on a quest for Quinosh.

*There was a hushed silence when Ammuma finished the story.*

*'Was Quila a ghost?' Molu asked softly, blinking her eyes.*

*'What makes you say that?'*

*'Dunno. The birds looked kinda scared.'*

*'We'll leave that to your interpretation,' Ammuma said tenderly.*

*Let's go on our jumbo trail to the forests of Kaziranga in Assam, famous for the ONE-HORNED RHINO.*

# Ruhi's Ruddy Rucksack

Ruhi woke up early, with an extra spring in her step. It was the *Kaziranga Kinetic Kiddos' Day*. Ruhi had signed up for the sack race.

'Why would you put yourself through that misery? What about weightlifting, or discus throw or any other sport where you don't have to stuff yourself in a sack and jump around?' Granny Radha said. She did not want to trample upon her grandcalf's dreams, but this was ridiculous!

'Let her try, Aayi,' Daddy Raj said. 'We don't want her to give up even before she starts. It's the spirit that counts.'

Raj and Rani arrived early to get a good spot in the grasslands of Kaziranga.

'Quite the crowd, eh?' Raj looked around and bobbed his 18-inch horn. It was heartening to see so many rhinos. Their population had increased in recent times. Humans were taking measures to protect them from being poached.

In the sack race camp were Gina the gaur, Babloo the bear and

SUNNY'S LOLLIES
KAZIRANGA KIN

Ruhi's friend Robby. What an assortment of participants!

The forest was filled with an air of festivity. Various stalls sold popular local snacks. A long line snaked to the stall where Gogoi Sunny the greater adjutant stork was selling his famous ice lollies. Word was that his flavours, like his species, were one of a kind. Ruhi would have loved to get hold of one of those luscious lollies but she had to focus on her technique. They were up next.

'On your marks. Get set. Go!'

Ruhi jumped forward with a firm push. She kept her balance in the rucksack. Gina had a clear lead. For a gaur, she was pretty agile. Ruhi could see Robby from the corner of her eye, snorting audibly with the effort of jumping. Suddenly Robby tripped over, falling flat on his nose. Ouch! That hurt.

Quick as a flash, Ruhi pulled up a dazed Robby saying, 'Come on. Let's do this together.' The crowd cheered the two as they hopped and grunted to the finish line, hand in hand.

Two surprises awaited Ruhi. A beaming granny Radha was waiting with open arms at the finish line. The second was an extra-large helping of Sunny's lollies!

As Ruhi's daddy said that morning, 'It's all about the spirit of the game!'

*'Who says no to ice lollies?' Molu asked in a shocked tone.*

*'Well, she got rewarded for her patience, didn't she?' Ammuma reminded her.*

*We move on to the snow-heavy mountains of Spiti Valley, in the Himalayan region, famous for the SNOW LEOPARD.*

# Sundari's Stunning Starlit Sky

Sundari looks at her reflection and purrs softly. She is the most beautiful snow leopard in the whole of Spiti. Her creamy fur, dotted with black rosettes*, forms geometric patterns right up to her bushy tail. She has perfect rings on her fur-cushioned paws that seem like designer snowshoes. Her rosy-pink nose and turquoise-blue eyes look like they have been moulded from the clear Himalayan stream, at the tip of the Gangotri glacier. Oh yes, she is beautiful but there is one problem. Sundari is lonely. She has no friends.

Sundari treads up to her favourite spot 18,000-feet high, overlooking Spiti Valley filled with rhododendrons, violet pansies and blue poppies. It's magical when the setting sun paints the sky with brilliant hues of purple, pink and indigo. It's a good spot to hunt for blue sheep, Sundari's favourite food. This is also the very spot they would play 'treasure hunt' and 'snowball' throws for hours. Sigh!

Sundari is lost in thought. She misses the fun times with her friends.

* resembling roses

'Flop!' A blob of ice smashes into Sundari's face. Who did that? She hears a chuffing from behind the snow-covered rock. It is Shalimar, her childhood friend, with whom she has played treasure hunt and snowball! He had left abruptly without saying goodbye. Shalimar approaches her. He has similar striking patterns on his fur but his eyes are an attractive emerald green!

'Peek-a-boo!' Sundari says and throws a snowball at him.

'Haha, Sundari, you remember.' Shalimar laughs, giving her a bouquet of pink and magenta azaleas.

'You remember too!' Sundari mews. They are her favourite wildflowers.

Nothing like laughing over funny childhood memories to break the ice. They catch up on the news. Shalimar explains that he left because food was getting scarce and his search for food had taken him far away.

Sundari and Shalimar watch the glorious sunset weave its enchanting spell in the Himalayan sky. The stars appear one by one, a twinkle here, a twinkle there until they gradually light up the skies. The snowflakes fall gently, blanketing the valley and turning Spiti into a winter wonderland. What a purr-fect day!

*'How come the snow leopards are endangered?' Kanna asked.*

*'Why was food getting scarce for Shalimar?' Molu wondered.*

*'That's what you will need to find out,' Ammuma said.*

*Now unfolds the tale of the BENGAL TIGER, deep in the jungles of Sunderbans in West Bengal.*

# Tej's Tiny Twist

Tej crouched stealthily, just as he had seen Ma do often. One false move and the jungle fowl would cluck away noisily. That would be the end of Tej's breakfast.

He was still smarting from his sisters' taunts. The only male in a litter of three, Tej was constantly teased by Tara and Tanvi. At six months, all three tigers had grown into remarkable beauties, each with their distinctive coats of orange and black stripes. When the sun's rays fell on them, it was as if they had their own spotlight. They shone like fire!

Tej wanted to prove to his sisters he could hunt as well as Ma. He crept away silently so as to not wake her up. The bamboo shoots by the tidal river provided the perfect cover. Apart from a few blabbering monkeys and his new buddy, the otter, there was no one around. A few days ago, straying into the marshes he had met Orup the otter. What fun they had together! When he got home, Ma spent an hour licking his coat clean, and then gave him a lecture on hygiene.

Orup waved to Tej, who waved back lifting his paw in an act of brotherhood. Big mistake. The rustling of the grass alerted the fowl who flew away clucking noisily. The monkeys cackled. Orup looked sheepish and Tej felt foolish. Uff!

'What do you think you're doing?' said his mother, Tejal. Her growl startled the cub. At once, the monkeys fell silent. Otto ducked behind the driftwood. Tejal looked fierce. Her eyes shone like burning candles and her canine teeth flashed like sharp knives when she growled.

'Ma … I almost caught it ... the monkeys distracted me,' stammered Tej feebly.

'You shouldn't be here on your own,' Tejal said. 'There are crocodiles in the river, cobras in the grass and ... anyway, I saw what you did. You are learning fast.'

Ma's words were like music to Tej's ears. What a twist!

'Let's go home, your sisters are waiting.'

Tej looked longingly at Orup. He was about to follow Ma, when she turned to him, and said, 'We'll come back later.'

Then she leapt like a bright flame into the mangrove foliage.

'I want to be strong like Ma when I grow up,' he thought, before jumping in after her.

*'Tyger, Tyger burning bright,*
*In the forests of the night* ...'*

*'OK, stop showing off,' Kanna interrupted Molu's recitation. 'Let's read the next story.'*

*'What's the hurry?' Molu was upset that Kanna had brushed aside her aha moment.*

*'It's the perfect poem for this story,' Ammuma acknowledged.*

---

* from *The Tyger* by William Blake

*Our jumbo trail beckons us to Sikkim, where we will meet the rare URSUS TIBETENUS, the white-chested bear.*

# Urvashi's Ups and Downs

Urvashi was annoyed with her brother Udit. Why had she listened to him? Now they were in for a real spanking from Mama Usha. It had started with Udit pestering Mama to let him go to River Teesta where he could feast on delicious berries. But Mama wouldn't dream of sending him alone.

'You are not ready to go off on your own, Udit,' she reasoned with him.

'I am. I'll stick to the path, grab a few berries, and return before sunset. Please, Mama,' Udit begged.

'On one condition: you'll return by afternoon and Urvashi will go with you.'

'What! Not Urvi. She'll slow me down and she whines a lot and …'

'Well then, your picnic will have to wait,' Usha cut short Udit's rant.

Udit gave in. Urvashi went berry-picking with her brother. Everything was going tickety-boo. They ate berries, nibbled on insects, made friends with Gemma, a rare green cochoa, and were heading back

home well in time. Then Udit lured Urvashi into the opposite trail with the promise of honey. The mention of honey made her smack her lips. *Slurp!*

'Follow me, it's not too far,' he said. And that's how they got into trouble. Three hours later, there was still no honey in sight. It was getting dark and the air was turning nippy. They were lost, tired, and scared of what Mama would say.

'It's your fault, Udit, you and your dimwit ideas,' moaned Urvashi, on the verge of tears. She was scared of running into wolves or snow leopards. Mama had warned them.

'Hello there! Aren't you Usha's twins?' hollered Rita the red panda.

'Yes,' they cried together.

'I recognized you by the V-shaped white patch on your chests. Looks like you are lost. Let me take you home.'

Rita pacified the two snivelling bear cubs and took them safe and sound to a much-relieved Usha, who looked like she had been crying too. She welcomed her cubs with big bear hugs and invited Rita to have dinner with them. The four enjoyed a hearty meal of shoots, assorted nuts and guess what else? Honey!

What a day of ups and downs, thought Urvashi!

*'A red panda! I wonder if they're really red?' Molu said.*

*Kanna whipped out his iPad to google the animal.*

*Ammuma suggested that they research the following morning. It was lights-out time.*

*Moving across from east to west, our next tale takes us to Phansad Wildlife Sanctuary, Maharashtra, to see WHITE-RUMPED VULTURES.*

# Varaz's Victory

Varaz was feeling hopeful and upbeat. Of late, conservation efforts to protect white-rumped vultures from going extinct had stepped up. Humans were seen milling around the area looking up treetops, and staring at him and his friends through long, black objects. Varaz's partner Vida had laid one egg that they both took turns to guard over until it hatched. The presence of their chick in the nest could also explain the flurry of human activity and interest.

Strange creatures, these humans. His mother Vana told him stories about how some humans considered vultures to be an important part of the cosmic transition of a departed soul.

'Hi Varaz! What's the latest on the snack scene?' hissed his pal Viraf, swooping down on the peepal tree next to him.

'There are remains of a wild buffalo, not far from here,' Varaz grunted.

'Great! I'll inform the others. Oh, and don't be late,' Viraf replied, beaming at his friend with the silvery bill and pink featherless head

before flying off.

Vultures feed on the flesh of dead animals. Unfortunately, over the years, Varaz noticed that his friends and relatives mysteriously fell ill and died soon after eating the carcass. Varaz had narrowly escaped death more than once. That's because he was always late for lunch!

Later, humans discovered that the cattle carcass carried a drug called diclofenac*. This may have caused the deaths of the vultures.

'Hiss, hiss, hiss,' the chick begged for food, while Vida made cooing sounds to calm it. 'Hush, my cupcake … Daddy's getting you a snack.'

'I'll be back soon,' Varaz called out as he soared in the sky, taking advantage of the wind currents. This time, he had to reach the wild buffalo carcass early.

Vida's thoughts went back to the times when they were troubled by lack of food and loss of habitat, but they always managed to overcome their difficulties and adapt. Lately, the vulture population has been on the rise because of a government initiative called Saving Asia's Vultures from Extinction (SAVE). That was a victory for Varaz and his fellow vultures!

She looked at her partner with pride. His large brown wings spanned 120 cm, each spread like Garuda's**. He glided effortlessly. He truly deserved the name Varaz, the one with great strength.

*'Varaz and Vida,' Molu said out loud. 'Are they Indian names, Ammuma?'*

*'Yes, they are Parsi names. Parsis are a group of people who follow Zoroastrianism. Their ancestors migrated from Persia, modern Iran.'*

*'I love their dish "dhansak". I had it once at my friend's birthday party,' Kanna added with a slurp.*

---

* anti-inflammatory drug used to treat pain and inflammation

** mythological bird

*In the far east, where the sun's rays first kiss the land of Arunachal Pradesh, we chase the tale of the WHITE-WINGED WOOD DUCK.*

# Wendy's Wise Words

Wendy wiggled her tail in glee. It was her babies' first day out. Six wonderful white-winged wood ducklings. Precious little pumpkins! Their heads were yellow with black feathers covering their tiny bodies. But soon they would get their mother's unique white head with black spots and patches of white on their wings. Would they have her red eyes or their father's orange eyes? Time would tell.

'Quack, quack!' Wendy called out in a reassuring voice as the six ducklings waddled behind, trying to keep up. She wobbled slowly, quacking and wiggling her tail so that they could follow her easily.

A few more steps and she would reach the clearing in the swamp. It was her favourite hideout – well shaded, plenty of tuck and isolated. Her babies could swim without any disturbance. With luck, she may even meet her dear friend Billy the Baer's pochard*. Wendy had saved Billy from being struck down once. She had quacked so wildly that Billy

* critically endangered bird

had been able to duck in time. One good deed deserves another. Billy had, in turn, alerted Wendy of a human trying to steal one of her eggs. They both exchanged notes on staying alive!

No sooner had Wendy and her chicks entered the grove than she heard a loud chorus. SURPRISE! The whole swamp was teeming with birds who had flown in from far and wide to congratulate her.

Wendy soon spotted Billy. Close to her was Heidi the hornbill. Then there were Feebi the fire-tailed myzornis and Gemma the gorgeous green cochoa from neighbouring Sikkim, chirruping in delight. Even Madhuri the Manipur bush quail had flown in. Wendy was overwhelmed. She burst into tears.

'Oh dear, I am at a loss for words,' she stuttered. 'I'm so grateful for your support. We must have each other's back if we are to survive in this world.'

'Wise words, Wendy,' they cheered.

'Cheep, cheep, cheep ...' The ducklings were in a hurry to swim. The swamp echoed with the twittering of joyful hope.

As Wendy led her ducklings into the river, the sky tied their dreams of a bright future with a rainbow-coloured ribbon.

*'I want to go birdwatching when I grow up,' Kanna said.*

*'Me too,' Molu hastily tagged.*

*'Noticed any familiar names?' Ammuma asked.*

*'I did. Bansi's friend Madhuri,' Molu said.*

*'And Gemma from Urvashi's tale,' Kanna added.*

*Hot on the jumbo trail is the XANTHOPHRYNE TIGERINA TOAD, also called Amboli toad, once again in the Western Ghats of Maharashtra.*

# Xini's Xylophone

'Xini ... spell amphibian for me.' Lulled by the afternoon heat, Xini had drifted into a trance, when his teacher's sharp croak snapped him out of his daydream.

'Xini, spell amphibian.' Ms Xeril's stern look was enough to turn anyone to stone.

Xini gulped. 'A-M-F-I—'

'Stop! You will croak the spelling 50 times as homework tonight and if you are caught dreaming one more time, I will make that a 100!' The sentence was pronounced and Ms Xeril sealed the declaration with a clucking of her throat.

Why did the English language have to be so difficult? Most of the words didn't sound the way they were spelt. All Xini had been dreaming of was the new xylophone he had got on his birthday.

Some giggles erupted from the females but they were squashed by Ms Xeril's icy stare. Poor Xini, always with his head in the clouds.

Xini was a rare species of toad, found only in the Amboli region of

Amboli Amphibian Academy

Maharashtra. He attended the Amboli Amphibian Academy, where it was practically impossible to get a toad leg in, let alone his long, sticky tongue. But Xini had a special talent. He could play the xylophone like a dream. That worked in his favour.

The air was getting unbearably humid. Without warning, the heavy-laden sky, bursting at its seams, exploded. These were showers of blessings on Xini and his toad mates, their clarion call!

'Class dismissed!' declared Ms Xeril and the entire academy erupted in one deafening 'Hurray!'

Toads hopped out of their classrooms leaping for joy as the rain lashed the earth. They splashed and skipped, jumped and croaked, in the hundreds of tiny puddles.

In the midst of this happy chaos, Xini found the perfect opportunity to play his xylophone. The moment was his to grab. You snooze, you lose, his father used to say. The merry sounds of toads, the rat-a-tat of the rain and Xini's tunes made a delightful orchestra.

♫ *'Ribbet-croak, pitter-patter, ting-a-ling-a-ling*
*Ribbet-croak, drip-drop, ting-a-ling-a-ling'* ♪

Xini played to his heart's content while his mates danced to the beat of his music.

Ms Xeril looked on admiringly. Xini had talent after all!

*'Haha, Xini sounds just like Kanna!' Molu burst into peals of laughter.*

*Kanna joined in the laughter. How well he could relate to Xini. He too had a tough time with spellings!*

*Our penultimate tale is set in the picturesque Pangong Tso (Lake) in Ladakh. Let's visit this scenic lake to see the YAKS.*

# Yakky Yuki's Yarns

Yuki was in the middle of a plot while munching breakfast when her mother called out to her. It was her turn to give rides to humans who came to visit the idyllic Pangong Tso. To pass the time, Yuki would cook up stories, lots of them, funny, bizarre, spooky. She entertained all the yaks in her town.

'Yuki, spin us a yarn,' her friends would say when she returned from the lake, and she would go yak, yak, yak. Where does she get all her ideas, her friends often wondered. Perhaps she gets inspired when she gazes upon the lake? Nestled in the Himalayan mountains at a height of 14,000 feet, Pangong Tso's blue waters sparkle when the dappled sunlight touches its surface. What a breathtaking sight! Perfect to plot and spin yarns.

Yuki was a favourite among the tourists. She was gentle and patient even when little humans tried to catch her bushy tail.

'I want to ride that one,' the tiny ones said, pointing to Yuki. 'Will she poke me if I touch her tail?' they asked.

That morning, moving to the far end of the lake, where multicoloured prayer flags fluttered in the wind, Yuki was surprised to find a new yak-face. Who is he, she wondered. The yak seemed at ease with humans, both locals and tourists. She heard the locals call him Yarzar. He had a shiny white coat with a striking red and blue square-patterned saddle over his broad back. Matching ribbons were tied at the tip of his long, sharp horns. A potential audience!

They exchanged looks with the promise of a beautiful friendship. Evening descended on Pangong Tso. Yuki and Yarzar gazed at the tranquil waters shimmering in the moonlight. Soothing chants could be heard from the distant monastery. A yellow wagtail perched on one of Yarzar's horns and pecked at his ribbons. Two brown-headed gulls glided in perfect symmetry and landed on the shore to peck at some crumbs.

Yuki felt a sense of calm as if she was one with the universe. She turned towards Yarzar who was leisurely chewing cud. It was time to spin one of her yarns.

'So, this blue sheep came to me the other day about a snow leopard … yak, yak, yak …'

*'Isn't it wonderful that each region in India has its unique names, customs, tradition, food and language?' Ammuma said as the story ended.*

*Molu was wondering what yarn Yuki would spin next.*

*We have reached the end of our jumbo trail. Our last stop is at Nellore in Andhra Pradesh, where the ZEBU breed of cattle is found.*

# Zesty Zara Zips

Zara tied the polka-dotted red scarf, that her mother Zukina had hand-stitched, around her neck. It was the morning of her graduation. She was called Zesty Zara because she loved outdoor activities – trekking, camping, birding. She was going to add three new activities to her list – zip-lining, zumba and zinnia planting!

Zara belonged to the rare zebu cattle breed. They have a distinctive hump on their shoulders which makes them look different from their bovine cousins. Some called it the fatty hump, some called it a beauty spot, but Zara called it a crown; it made her look like a princess!
She was admiring herself in the mirror when a croaky sound at the doorstep brought her out of her vanity mode.

'Zara, look who's come to wish you,' called out her mom Zukina.

Zara zipped to her porch. 'Ziggy!' she squealed in delight. 'How nice of you to visit.' The Zakerana Murthii or the Ghats wart frog is an endangered species found in the Western Ghats, near Karnataka.

'You're our special guest. Please attend the graduation,' Zukina said.

Once the certificates had been awarded, it was time for Ms Zachariah, the oldest and kindest teacher in the village, to address the gathering.

'This bountiful Earth has plenty of room and resources for all creatures big and small. Destroy less, conserve more. Scorn less, care more. Take less, give more. Let us nurture and nourish all life. Let us learn to share space with humans and live in harmony. Remember, *one planet, many species, one life, many dreams, one step, many leaps!*'

Ms Zachariah ended her speech by stressing the last word with a stomp of her hoof. That must have triggered it. At the mention of the word 'leaps', Ziggy leapt onto the podium and landed on Ms Zachariah's hump! From his aerial view, Ziggy could see the audience staring at him. Had he missed something?

Afterwards, the family had a hearty laugh over that afternoon's fiasco. Ms Zachariah brushed aside the incident claiming that her words had made a mark!

That night, Zara reflected on Ms Zachariah's closing lines, with a deep sense of gratitude. She had so much to do and she could do anything her heart desired. The world was her oyster! She had to start zipping!

*Ammuma finished the last story with a flourish. The room was suffused with the warm glow of the moonlight and the heady fragrance of jasmine. The racket of the crickets' chirp had dimmed to a murmur.*

*'Wow!' Kanna said softly. 'So many endangered species of animals and birds all over India. I think I'm going to work in the forests when I grow up.'*

*'I must also start zipping,' Molu said excitedly.*

*'And yakking too,' Kanna added tongue-in-cheek.*

*'Molu, do you remember you asked what we were doing to protect these animals?' Ammuma reminded her.*

*'Yeah, you said that people are helping a lot, but more needs to be done.'*

*'There you go. You too can contribute to those conservation efforts when you grow up.'*

*Ammuma knew in her heart that Kanna and Molu would leave the village richer in thought and action.*

*10 p.m. Lights-out time. She bid them goodnight and gently closed the bedroom door. Kanna and Molu were tucked into their beds, lost in their own jungle world. A sleep fairy was bouncing about their eyelids, but a flicker outside the window made her vanish. Fireflies! Again! This time the children watched them dance until the sleep fairy returned and cast a magical spell on them. Kanna and Molu drifted into a deep slumber with stories swirling in their minds.*

*In the distance, the jungles continued to whisper.*

# Moving Around the Magical Map

- Asian elephant
- Bengal florican
- King cobra
- Ganges river dolphin
- Steppe eagle
- Anaimalai flying frog
- Gharial
- Hangul, the red stag
- Indian/Asiatic lion
- Jenkins's shrew
- Kala hiran
- Lion-tailed macaque
- Mouse deer
- Nilgiri tahr
- Olive ridley turtle
- Peacock
- Himalayan quail
- One-horned rhino
- Snow leopard
- Bengal tiger
- Ursus Tibetenus
- White-rumped vulture
- White-winged wood duck
- Xanthophryne tigerina toad
- Yak
- Zebu cattle

## Fun Facts of Faunal Friends

*The* **ASIAN ELEPHANT** *uses its feet to hear sounds.*

*The* **BENGAL FLORICAN** *is a bird that is adapted for walking, but can fly long distances too.*

*A* **KING COBRA'S** *bite is so poisonous that it can even kill an elephant!*

*A* **DOLPHIN** *can navigate and hunt using echolocation.*

*One of the fastest birds in the world, the* **STEPPE EAGLE** *can fly up to 60 km.*

*The* **ANAIMALAI FLYING FROG** *is also known as the false Malabar gliding frog.*

*The male* **GHARIAL** *sports a large growth on its snout called a ghara, the Hindi word for 'mud pot'.*

*A subspecies of the elk, a* **HANGUL** *has spots on its body when it is a fawn.*

*The* **INDIAN/ASIATIC LION** *is smaller than the African lion. Its mane grows on the top of its head, so its ears are visible.*

*The* **JENKINS'S SHREW** *is tiny with very dense fur.*

*The* **KALA HIRAN** *or the blackbuck can run faster than any predator, except the cheetah.*

*The* **LION-TAILED MACAQUE** *has a long tail with a tuft of black hair at the end resembling a lion's tail, hence the name.*

*The* **MOUSE DEER** *is the only type of deer without antlers.*

*The name* **NILGIRI TAHR** *comes from Neelagiri meaning 'blue hills' in Tamil and trágos meaning 'goat' in Greek.*

*The* **OLIVE RIDLEY TURTLE** *has the ability to sleep underwater for about two hours without surfacing for air.*

*A* **PEACOCK** *has a pretty crest on its head which actually acts as a sensor.*

*The* **HIMALAYAN QUAIL** *has not been sighted for more than 125 years! The quest is still on ...*

*The* **RHINO**, *although bulky, is quick-footed and can charge up to 30 miles an hour when it is angry.*

*A* **SNOW LEOPARD** *does not roar! It only chuffs, growls, hisses and mews!*

*Just like zebras, no two* **TIGERS** *have the same stripes. They are unique like human fingerprints!*

*The* **URSUS TIBETENUS** *or white-chested bear can walk in a vertical position for a quarter of a mile!*

*A* **VULTURE** *soars by making use of rising columns of warm air called 'thermals'. What a clever way to use natural energy!*

*The* **WHITE-WINGED WOOD DUCK** *has a ghostly call. Due to this peculiar sound, it is called 'Deo Hans' in Assamese, meaning spirit duck.*

*The male* **XANTHOPHRYNE TIGERINA TOAD**, *also called Amboli toad, has bright yellow skin, marked with light to dark brown stripes. That's why it's also called 'tiger toad'.*

*The* **YAK** *can survive in temperatures as cold as -40 degrees Celsius.*

*The* **ZEBU** *stores food in its hump, like the camel, for use in case of need.*

The following images are from Wikimedia Commons.
page 28, STEPPE EAGLE
page 37, HANGUL
page 67, RHINO

# INDEX

# AUTHOR'S NOTE

This book is a tribute to the relentless work of conservationists to protect and preserve endangered species in India. It is also to encourage children to be aware of and appreciate our rich faunal diversity. Who knows, they might be inspired to contribute towards these conservation measures when they grow up.

My heartfelt gratitude to Dr Ullas Karanth and Mr Romulus Whitaker, who read my stories, gave invaluable inputs and validated my endeavour. My sincere thanks to Dr Raju Kasambe, whose insight on critically endangered birds helped me refine my stories. Neena Mehrotra was the first to proofread and provide constructive feedback all through. I'm grateful to Jayaprakash Satyamurthy, Aditi Pant and Divya Mehrotra for their perspective, and my family for encouraging my imagination to take flight.

A big shout-out to the illustrators who brought each endangered species to life with their strokes and brushes. Parvathy Subramaniam, Tanisha Tiwari, Mukund Ravishankar, Tayyibah Kazim, Krithika Ramesh, Vibha Jayaram and Saswati Patra spent many painstaking hours creating these delightful illustrations. Thank you, Divya Menon, my niece, for the beautiful front and back cover, capturing the wonder of children.

My characters jump with joy, sigh in relief, cry with worry, chuckle in jest, pine for loss, sulk in envy, and do much more just like us. All that remains is for you to read these stories to or along with your little ones so that they can visualize and enjoy the magic of these precious animals and birds in our jungles.

## *About the Author*

Preethi Menon is an educator, with more than three decades of teaching experience. She was born, raised and schooled in Kuwait. Her higher education was from various institutions in Kerala. Preethi has taught in schools in Mumbai, Vizag, Delhi and Wellington (Coonoor). She has been teaching in different international schools in Bengaluru for the last seventeen years. She loves travelling and is passionate about nature and wildlife. She enjoys birdwatching and has been to many of the forest reserves mentioned in the book.

## *About the Illustrators*

Parvathy Subramanian is an illustrator based out of Chennai who loves to make you chuckle with her drawings about animals and humans living in urban areas. In this book, she has illustrated Chandrika the king cobra, Freddie the Anaimalai flying frog, Jancy the Jenkins's shrew and Kuldeep the kala hiran.

Tanisha Tiwari is an artist and a designer based in Bengaluru. She calls herself a 'cat-crazy' person. She has illustrated Anju the elephant, Bansi the Bengal florican, Divya the Gangetic dolphin, Eklavya the steppe eagle and Izzy the Indian/Asiatic lion,

Mukund Ravishankar hails from Coonoor. Being in the midst of natural beauty, Mukund's illustrations capture the beauty of hills effortlessly. He has drawn murals of wildlife across Coonoor town. He has illustrated Meera the mouse deer, Nimmi the Nilgiri tahr, Ruhi the rhino, Sundari the snow leopard, Tej the Bengal tiger, Urvashi the white-chested bear and Wendy the white-headed wood duck.

Saswati Patra is a Bengaluru-based freelance artist. She has hand-painted Hasan the handsome hangul and Prem the peacock.

Krithika Ramesh is an architect from Coonoor who has won the Vajra World Records for carving the letters A to Z on a microtip. Krithika has illustrated Quila the mystical and elusive Himalayan quail.

Vibha Jayaram is a Bengaluru-based freelance illustrator and artist. Her illustrations include the characters Onjali the turtle, Varaz the vulture, Xini the toad, Yuki the yak and Zara the zebu cow.

Tayyibah Kazim, my ex-student and the first illustrator for this book, is a second-year student in Communication and Journalism in Northwestern University, Qatar. Tayyibah did the illustrations of Gowri the gharial and Lila the lion-tailed macaque.

Divya Menon from Coonoor is an Early Years educator and a certified yoga instructor. She is also the founder of Volunteers of Nilgiris, a group of eco-warriors who carried out hill clean-ups and awareness campaigns on anti-littering and waste management. She's a self-taught artist who enjoys painting nature. Divya has made the front and back cover pages of this book.